HERO HAVOC!

BANTAM BOOKS

Bizarro lives on
a strange planet
called Bizarro World.

4

Bizarro wants to be
like his hero,
Superman.

But Bizarro is
Superman's opposite.
He always gets
things wrong.

The "S" on Bizarro's chest is backwards.

Superman flies
straight and fast.

But Bizarro flies
crooked and slow.

Superman's heat vision
can cut through anything.

Bizarro has freeze vision.

BRRRR!

Superman's super-breath cools off hot volcanoes.

But watch out . . .

Bizarro breathes fire!

Bizarro sees Earth.

He has an idea!

He will visit

the Super Friends.

They will show him
how to be a hero!

Bizarro lands
in Metropolis.
CRUNCH!
He stops the Penguin.

"Bizarro wants to be a hero," he says. "Me make good start!" (Bizarro talks funny, too.)

The Super Friends
will teach Bizarro.

Batman is quiet
when catching the
bad guys.

But Bizarro is loud!

The Flash is fast
when stopping
the bad guys.

Bizarro is slow –
but he still stops
the bad guys!

Green Lantern always helps people in need.

Bizarro tries to help.

But he makes mistakes.

Bizarro flies off
to find Superman.
The Super Friends
follow him.

Lex Luthor has
Superman.
He is chained up
with Kryptonite.

The green rock
makes Superman weak.
Bizarro races to help.

Bizarro breaks the chains,
takes the Kryptonite . . .

. . . and throws it
far into space!

Superman is saved!
He makes a gift
for Bizarro.

"You may be different,"
Superman says,
"but today you are
my hero."

Bizarro heads home.
He is happy because
he is a real hero!